This book is dedicated to kind and courageous children everywhere.

READER

An Open Letter to Parents and Teachers:

Like all *Short Vowel Adventures*, **Hop, Frog!** highlights
one short vowel sound, in this case the short "o" sound.
We believe this phonics focus helps beginning readers gain
skill and confidence. After the story, we've included two
Story Starters, just for fun. *Story Starters* are open-ended
questions that can be used as a jumping-off place for
conversation, storytelling, and imaginative writing.

At BraveMouse Books we believe the most important
part of any reading program is the shared experience of
a good story. We hope you'll enjoy **Hop, Frog!**
with a child you love!

The BraveMouse Team

Hop, Frog!

by Molly Coxe

BraveMouse Readers

Brave
Mouse
Books

Tick. Tock.
Six o'clock.
Time for the
hopping contest!

Ready, set, **HOP!**

Frog hops.

Frog stops
to help his friend Pollywog.

"Thanks, Frog,"
says Pollywog.
"No prob!" says Frog.

Frog hops.

Frog stops
to help his friend Fox.

"Thanks, Frog,"
says Fox.
"No prob!" says Frog.

Frog hops.

Frog stops
to help his friend Ox.

"Thanks, Frog!"
says Ox.
"No prob!" says Frog.

Frog hops.

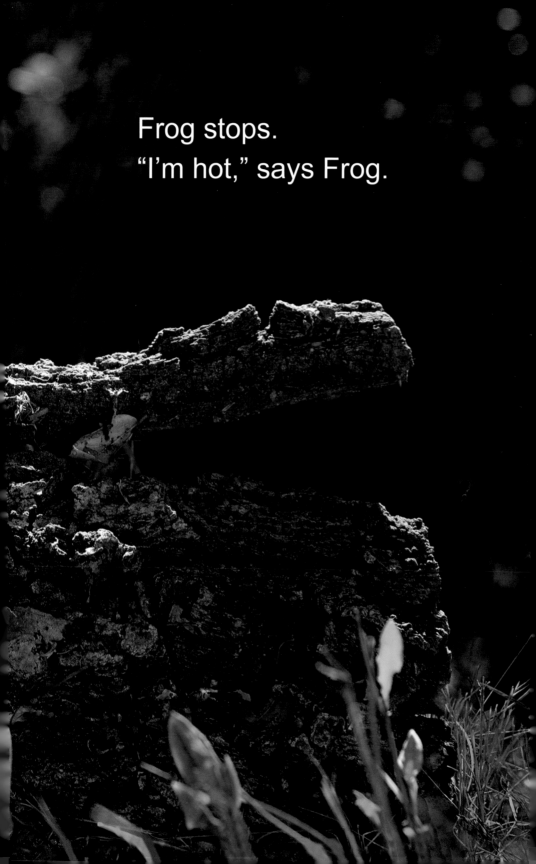

Frog stops.
"I'm hot," says Frog.

Too hot. Too hot to hop!
"Frog needs help!"
says Pollywog.

Frog's friends carry Frog.

They all win
the hopping contest.

"Thank you, friends!"
says Frog.
"No prob, Frog!"

Story Starters

Pollywog is on a log.
Where will she go?

What do Mom and Tom
see in the fog?